TOO TALL

Written by
Karen Gerald Wheaton

Illustrated by
Adam Smith

Too Tall
©1999 Wright Group Publishing, Inc.
By Karen Gerald Wheaton
Illustrated by Adam Smith

Breakthrough to Literacy™
©1998 Wright Group Publishing, Inc.

The Wright Group
19201 120th Avenue NE
Bothell, WA 98011
www.WrightGroup.com

Printed in Canada

10 9 8 7 6 5 4 3 2

ISBN: 0-322-01530-8
ISBN: 0-322-01605-3 (6-pack)

Giant was big and strong
but Giant was not very happy.

Giant had trouble playing
with the kids on his block.

Their skateboards were too skinny.

Their swings were too small.

Their bikes were too little.

Giant was just too tall.

He tried to jump on trampolines.

He even played baseball.

Whatever Giant tried to do,

he always felt too tall.

Then one day it happened...

while leaning on a tree.

A little girl began to climb...

first one, then two, now three.

Soon all the kids were climbing.

Giant held them all.

At last the big, strong giant
was glad to be too tall.